For Benedicte Barford and Stephanie Amster
with love and thanks Emma

ORCHARD BOOKS

338 Euston Road, London NW1 3BH

Orchard Books Australia

Level 17/207 Kent Street, Sydney, NSW 2000

First published in 2009 by Orchard Books
First published in paperback in 2010

ISBN 978 1 84616 995 3

A CIP catalogue record for this book
is available from the British Library.

10 9 8 7 6 5 4 3 2 1

Printed in China

Orchard Books is a division of
Hachette Children's Books,
an Hachette UK company.
www.hachette.co.uk

I don't want a cool cat

Emma Dodd

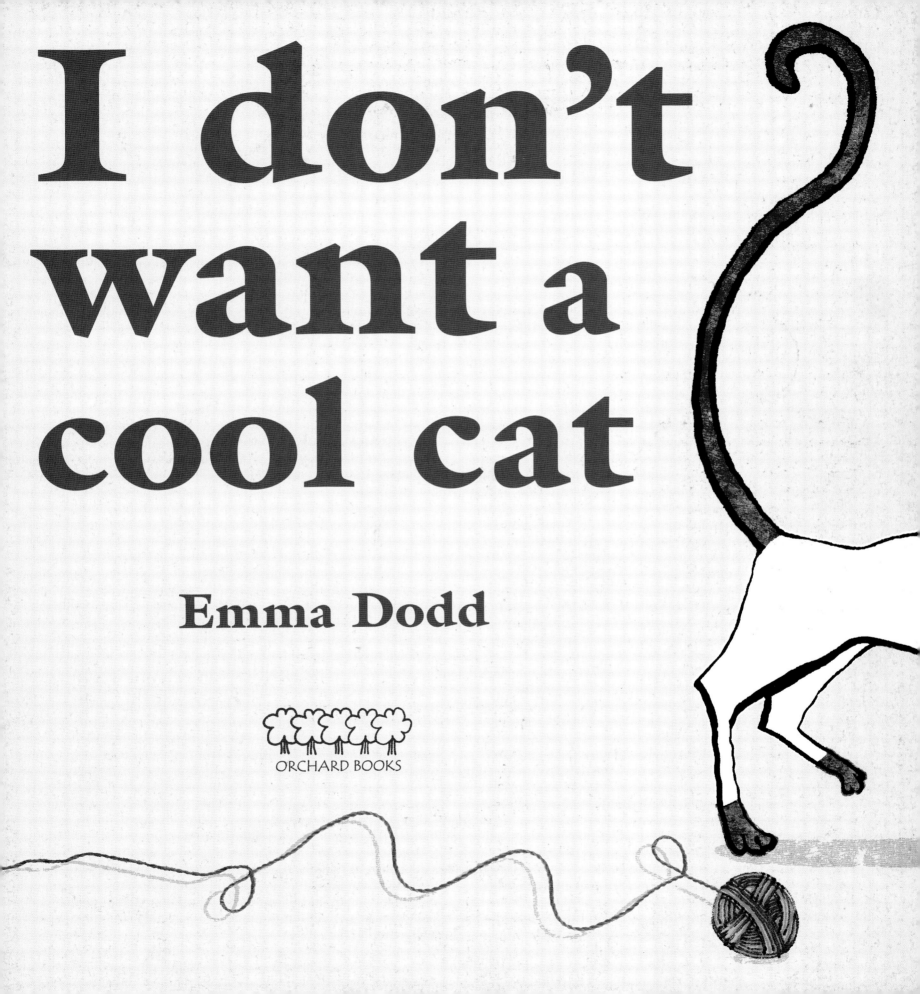

ORCHARD BOOKS

I don't want

a cool cat.

A treat-me-like-a-fool cat.

I don't want a stuffy cat.

A huffy, over-fluffy cat.

I don't want a night cat.

A looking-for-a-fight cat.

I **don't want** a greedy cat.

A "Miaow, miaow, please feed me" cat.

I don't want a
prize cat.

The best-that-money-buys cat.

A howly, yowly,
scowly cat.

I don't want

a big cat.

Or a slinky,
dinky, twig cat.

I just want

a purry cat.

A small,
soft,
furry cat.

Not a scratch or scrap cat.
A curl-up-in-my-lap cat.

A glad

when

I come

home cat.

A cat I can call

My Own Cat.